INTERMEZZO IN BARCELONA

Cristina Roldán

BALBOA.PRESS
A DIVISION OF HAY HOUSE

Balboa Press books may be ordered through booksellers or by contacting:

Balboa Press
A Division of Hay House
1663 Liberty Drive
Bloomington, IN 47403
www.balboapress.com
1 (877) 407-4847

Interior Image Credit: Cristina Roldán
Cover Image Credit: Cristina Roldán/Mariah Rodriguez

Print information available on the last page.

ISBN: 978-1-9822-4566-5 (sc)
ISBN: 978-1-9822-4567-2 (e)

Balboa Press rev. date: 04/07/2020

CONTENTS

THE RETURN

"Bring me sweet words, let them become the roots of my life; let whoever can, arrive. If my father and mother must die, I have to find the amulet that amulet that gives life."

Juan José Rebabarrive (1903, Antananarivo)
(Excerpt from old songs from the country of Imerina)

This work is the result of imagination of the author. Any resemblance to people or facts of reality will be pure coincidence. If you have no put something similar you must to do it.Thank you.

Best regards
Cristina Roldan

ONE: A VULGAR STORY

There was something squalid that linked me to this chaotic city from Las Ramblas to the high part of the city where I lived, with its profligates — some unkempt and greasy-haired — who passed by one another without a glance as if on their way to nowhere.

I took a deep breath through the car window and then heard how — in the far distance — my heartbeats sought their rhythm. The sky was a bluish grey, but not entirely, as though it also needed a coat of paint or a good cleaning.

"It's a diabolical city", I said to myself, and kept driving in the midst of a hell jam-packed with people and cars that — by some miracle — managed to avoid running into each other. To my left, the promenade with its cafés, birds and flowers. The agglomeration of people strolling back and forth. Tania, on my right, seemed impassive. I looked at her out of the corner of my eye. How is it possible that she does not figure it out? I smiled at her while the traffic light was red; she gave me a peck on the cheek. "Home at last, mum!" I started the car. The light was green again, but we moved with the flow, as if we were walking; there were a lot of cars. We had just left the boat and I already missed the sky of the Balearic Islands and Palma's air, so clean, blue and very high, so different than that of my hometown… Las Ramblas never ended. It was almost nine o'clock at night towards the end of August. People had just stepped out for a stroll before dinner and it took us a good half hour to get to the Plaza de Cataluña. "At the end of the day, you were born here, Maria", I said to myself. "You belong to this landscape, you should feel more of a connection." "Yes, but I don't want to", I answered myself in a silent monologue. I thought about him. The years had passed, but he surely had strolled through these places, although, in essence, few things have changed. My mouth tasted sour from the seasickness pills I had taken during the day. Perhaps I had been wrong. Perhaps it was false. I had made false excuses about my staying in Barcelona despite...

Maybe I could get away because — deep down — I was closely tied to the city and that more profound (but objectively unknown) reasons had me tied to that kind of area that enwraps me, perhaps it's that..., but then… I was lying to myself? How is that I wasn't honest even with myself?

I rejected this thought while we crossed the Paseo de Gracia; it was truly a bad time for cheap philosophy.

This trip that weighs on my heart here, next to my stomach, right here, grating, and here again... at home again?

We hop into bed and I try to adjust my body to the new mattress. The sheets were clean and smelled slightly of must mixed with vervain. I asked Tania something; she did not answer and her deep breathing told me she was already asleep. Suddenly, the phone began to ring. Quite insistently. Groping in the dark, I rolled out of my trundle bed and sat down on the edge. The wood pressing sharply into my buttocks, I picked up the phone. "Yes?, yes?" I said, while looking at my little wristwatch. Hours had passed while I was asleep; the hands said it was ten past three. At the other end of the telephone, no one... I turned back to my pillow. I was beginning to fall back asleep when it rang again. This time I had time enough to answer. But, once again, silence. I reacted, telling myself, "It could not have come from outside; phone calls inevitably go through reception or from room to room". I dialled reception. The concierge told me that he knew nothing about it and to leave the phone off the hook. So I did. I fell right back asleep.

TWO: A TRIP TO THE PAST

The day dawned furiously beautiful. The sky was blue and so was the swimming pool. Tania and I were outsiders on Mallorca at the Beach apartments, where the clientele, menus, schedules and parties were all German. The local native waitstaff spoke the language flawlessly and the menus were written exclusively in German. Tonight, I saw and heard them. We were coming back from a stroll through the town, after dinner, when we hear them sing. They sounded like a church choir. Tania was playing with a little *gadget* we had bought in a tourist shop and I followed the sound coming from not so far away. My footsteps were guided by it through a corridor that led to a closed door; the singing was louder. It sounded like an old Teutonic song or some kind of Wagnerian chorus.

Without thinking twice, I opened the door, but only halfway. A large Nazi Swastika drawn on a white sheet presided over the room and the singers had a cross painted on the armband they wore on their right arms. I closed the door and I went to find to Tania. The next day at the pool, my daughter was playing on a rubber raft in its very blue water while I lay back on the lounge chair, singing softly and enjoying the sunshine. There was a couple — well past middle-aged — to our right and when the man headed to the pool, hit my chair with his foot and knocked it over. I could not help but feel bad because he did not even apologise. Later on, we sat down at small tables near the pool under some umbrellas to eat. It was packed with people who were also eating. Children played by dumping their pails on the ground. The *headwaiter* reproved Tania for dirtying the floor with her wet bikini. She let him know that it had been the pails of the nearby children. He fell silent and said nothing to the children who continued emptying their pails. Later, when he served us breakfast, he did not put on a tablecloth, as he did on the other tables. Piqued with curiosity, I asked him about it. His face turned red, said he was not racist, and walked away. Frankly, I did not understand his irony at all. We continued enjoying the sun and sea.

THREE: THE PAST THAT DOES NOT CHANGE

Don Ceferino was a character who — due to his appearance — could serve as an illustration in a manual for respectable men: conservative clothing; neutral, never loud, colours and the same for the shoes; and classic and sober-coloured ties. Friendly smile, subtle, moderate conversation, facile of speech, quick and flexible in his responses. Life had been a slow safe "climb", or upwards path, in a career that had been meticulously planned, designed, step by step. He would have never imagined that he would have gone as far has he had when he left Martos, his hometown.

Don Ceferino was eleven when he decided that when the finished the normal school where he studied, he would study to be a lawyer. Yes, he was going to be a lawyer.

He admired these people, these gentlemen in pristine white suits and traditional bone-coloured straw hats (like the ones from Havana in the early twentieth century). He watched them through the casino's window while he played dominos, sometimes with a Havana cigar in his right hand and always with a small thin glass in front, on the table on which his elbows rested lightly.

It was the judge who impressed Ceferino most, and his head began to fill with great dreams. Because Ceferino Domínguez del Ciervo was from a family poor in money — "of modest means", so to speak — but of spotlessly untarnished reputation. He was the third of five siblings, four boys and a girl. His father worked as a secretary in the town hall and his mother did housework. He was the apple of his mother's eye. When he was small, he returned her love with affection and when he was older, he treated her with great kindness.

In 1921, Martos was a largish white village that was growing towards the mountain, upwards. The only thing that all the townsfolk knew about its story was that the rock that fell from above had borne witness to the battle between the two Mozarab brothers, as the legend — which the priest knew by heart — told.

The town was a fine example of the saying that goes "Martos, untamed city of a thousand taverns and not a single bookshop". This was strictly true. The main wealth came from the olive trees managed by two gentlemen who, though they owned local farms, continued residing in Madrid and with flats in Jaen. The latter was not far away, but reaching it required taking a winding road full of endless silvery olive trees planted to the left and right.

When he reached puberty, Ceferino — almost Don Ceferino by now — befriended Preñaceta, a painter from Martos with a certain renown in Madrid. In the capital, she garnered some attention in artistic circles for her expressionist painting, a style not fully accepted in the Spain of the time.

It was during those years that the young Ceferino began to make his way with the particular character of the young Andalusian gentleman. This was not due to property and money, but actually because he was attracted by sexual pleasures that were heavily repressed because of his mother. She was devoted to the Virgin of the Rule, and Ceferenito always wore a medal with her image on it over her heart. He also had — very deep inside, but with an incessant force — the ability to rise, to achieve, power. He still did not know how, but he had already learnt from an early age, that in Spain, power was related to decency, good manners and restraint, the modesty of respectable men, women in black with their rosaries, and that Mass every day was a synonym of virtue, where all pleasures were conducted behind closed doors, where people knew. He also knew about the private parties of strongmen and the pampered sons of the rich, and the homosexual deviations of many of them. But it was taboo to mention it, make a comment, turn it into words and even more so — God save us — to put it into words on paper.

When Ceferino was studying for the civil service exams, at sunset he would often climb the stairway to the Peñafreta's workshop. He would spend hours there talking with don José Maria about painting and art in general. Their meetings were full of moments to savour and dreams shared by both. It got to the point that their friendship, their relationship, turned more subtle and the looks... the unexpected touches, would remain hidden forever between the four walls that surrounded them. The reality is that — after more than 35 years — these tendencies or contacts might have been real and could have ended up manifesting themselves differently, perhaps in the sexual expressiveness of Don Ceferino, by now residing in Barcelona and converted into a good-looking seventy-something pensioner. He had had several triumphs in his career. He was a mature man, of irreproachable appearance, conservative and quite well cared for. In his youth, Ceferinito was attracted to the visual arts in general (as we mentioned earlier) and had a particular interest in painting and in poetry. In his middle age, he went on to publish a number of scripts, collections of poetry and episodes from his life as a student to launch his legal career. He also exchanged letters with the friend from his younger days, the painter Peñafreta.

FOUR: THE PAST THAT ALWAYS RETURNS

Tania and I finished our tennis game. I was tired of picking up the balls, as I was no Ivan Lendl or anything close. We set out to close the gate to the tennis court and return to our little apartment. It was about eight o'clock in the evening and night was beginning to fall. Following the small path from the upper part of Paguera, I was hurrying towards the hotel (Tania had gone on ahead to shower first) when I noticed a hand was grabbing me while something — maybe a foot or leg — made me stagger until I fell flat on the ground. I felt the blades of grass stabbing my legs and, suddenly, he was at my flanks, on top of me. He ripped off *my pants* and penetrated at once. I tried to scream, but something like a wet handkerchief stopped me. I felt his hot milk inside me like a pipe and I relaxed, suddenly thinking about those articles I had read about consented rape, but… what could I do? Although my throat was choked with disgust, my stomach was like plasterboard, like something that stopped me from vomiting. The minutes went by and, suddenly, I realised that he was gone. I got up, pulled down my shirt and, without thinking, picked up the tennis balls that had fallen out of their storage box, counting them, "One, two, three … one's missing. Here it is, near the pine tree".

When I entered the room, Tania was still in the shower and I quickly thought about going to the police station. I had heard about semen analyses and so on. Tania came out wrapped in a towel. "Wow, look at your hair, mummy." I spontaneously decided to shower, just like that. I think I was under the warm water for a half hour; I did not feel clean. A strange smell in me penetrated my skin; it was sour and unpleasant, and stubbornly persisted. I put on some Nenuco cologne; I showered it on and we got dressed and went down for dinner.

There he was in the dining room, hair in place and properly dressed — quite well put together — sitting calmly at his usual table, eating by his wife.

Later, after night had fallen and my daughter was sleeping, the tears came and rolled down my cheeks. They came out hot and calm, slipping down my cheek, moderate at first, but later they suddenly took hold of me, filling my chest with rage and indignation.

FIVE: ANOTHER TURN OF THE CRANK

The decade of the fifties was in full swing when Don Ceferino Dominguez del Ciervo went to Barcelona. He had been named judge and had a certain reputation which had been solidly and skilfully earned in Madrid. There had been hard years, years of study and work, and changes, too, in both his family and professional lives. His mother, his sainted mother, had died suddenly. Ceferino did not have enough time to reach her while she was still alive. All he could do was race from Cuenca — where he was posted — to see her in her wooden box and accompany her to the burial.

Her memory would accompany him his entire life. Some of his brothers had stayed in the town. The eldest drowned on a beach in Cadiz, carried away by the undertow. He was careful — he did not know how to swim, just the dead-man's float — but, when he realised what was going on, he lost his footing and, shortly thereafter, his life. His father, left paraplegic from his attacks, lived with his sister Jesusa in Jaen. She had married a secondary school teacher and she herself gave private tuition. His other brothers had also established themselves in that city. As for their country home, it had been left empty, locked and shuttered tightly.

Don Ceferino thought that the time had come for him to marry. After two years in Barcelona, he set his sagacious eyes on a young woman whose attraction was more financial than physical. A little Catalan slut, who grabbed on to the string of the ball Ceferino had tossed her guided more by his head than his heart. He did it with prudence, like everything that had ruled his life so far, levering it in his career, a primary goal set in his childhood and in the spirit and thinking of this man who used his increasingly limited free time to write a little poetry.

He had set aside being a producer of paintings, though not being a novice patron of them. On a daily basis, he cultivated more contact with artists from the Ateneo de Barcelona and elsewhere, mainly supporting beginning avant-garde artists.

His paraplegic father died, leaving Jesusa to finally rest. She was able to be the matron of honour at his wedding with Montserrat, as his fiancée was called. The wedding took place in the Church of Our Lady of Mercy and was considered an event in the small social circle in which Don Ceferino moved. But the years passed and the family would soon increase considerably. After the first year, Ceferinito was born. Don Ceferino had no concerns about money, since Maria Montserrat — Montse to friends and family — had married him under a community property arrangement so that he, who was experienced in legal matters, could manage her fortune for her; she was an orphan, the only heir and did not know how – or was not able to – due to the old tradition based on the deeply rooted idea in Spain that beauty is incompatible with intelligence. So, she should have been smart, but — despite having a lively character and being as jealous as they come — while not being (let us be honest) actually stupid, she was definitely not brilliant. Lucidity is not what would set Monserrat Treseras apart. An ample flat on the Diagonal; an office in the highest part of the city, and another, more private one, on Aragon Street. A district prosecutor, Don Ceferino's career was rocketing upwards when his second son, Fernandito, was born.

During this period, the couple — with regard to sex — was already in a phase of deep discord and clear lack interest. Montserrat, who was concerned with gossip and appearances, seized upon the idea of persevering and saving their marriage, "whatever it takes and whatever the cost". This was fine with Don Ceferino, who in the fifties had already had innumerable flings; he was an expert in political reactions and navigating them without getting wet with exemplary skill and mastery. He moved up quickly and ended up as president of the Supreme Court. First, and then he was appointed the President of the General Council of the Judiciary by the Socialists. This title offered him multiple perks from people who played up to him and looked upon him with respect. He had made it. The dream of that boy who had left Martos, who had always desired power; now he had it. And he wielded it from a safe place that he knew how to handle with incredible skill, mindful and always familiar with his interlocutor. Oh, if his mother could only see him! How proud Virtudes would be of him! He, however, proud of being an obviously pragmatic man, agnostic and cold, had a hidden hope — which he himself did not admit — that his sainted mother could see him from somewhere, some place, and that she would be smiling at the sight of Ceferinito having become much more than just an "honourable judge".

Well into the eighties, Ceferino Dominguez held the highest post in the judiciary and had been successful; he had achieved his childhood ambitions. He was successful in the full sense of the word. Over a period of several years, he prepared his retirement, having been able to keep his head above water better than anyone else during the difficult path of transition from Franco's dictatorship to democracy and socialism. Afterwards, it was Ceferino — or Ceferinito — since he had always remained faithful to his childhood ambitions. Time kept passing. Don Ceferino stayed faithful to his principles of being loyal to whatever system was best for him. Now, his contacts were the country's most elite politicians and he felt comfortable in the life he had built based on a skilfully drawn line. Nothing had come from improvisation; quite the contrary.

AUTHOR'S ASIDE BETWEEN CHAPTERS FIVE AND SIX

In his ripe old age, Don Ceferino had become fond of orgies — which he called festivals — and which he organised in his office at the end of the day, when the clients had left. He usually had one every four or five months. His body — reduced by ageing — could do no more. Naive thirty-something couples like, for instance, Marta y José had fallen into his trap. José needed more money and Marta, his wife, needed a job. They were accompanied by Catalina, an aspiring actress, a drug addict who never stopped laughing at their little parties while she spread her legs and allowed herself to be taken by José, who was getting ready to set upon her. Meanwhile, Don Ceferino was giving Marta a good going over, laid out on towels arranged on the carpet. He adjusted the framed mirror on the wall so he could see the other couple, but could not avoid the early ejaculation he had had since puberty. While José, whose eyes were filled with tears as his wife cheated on him — with his consent — did not try to make it with Catalina, who laughed endlessly. Don Ceferino — drooling, out of it, dry, with pallid, grey skin and a limp dick, paraded about naked and without shame, feeling like a king. But this was not enough for José and Marta, the Martís, when they found out that the only perk they would get was a book like the ones that banks give you for opening an account. After four or five of these parties, they quit, leaving Don Ceferino without his fun, as his wife kept a close eye on the money and he could not afford a real party with professionals. And so the Martís walked down the stairs with the book full of publicity about the bank. The first day, Marta, had avidly — uselessly — searched for a bank note or a cheque among its pages, saying, "This is the last time", while Catalina laughed and laughed. Some months later, the actress died of AIDS in Hospital del Mar, one of the first cases in Barcelona. Don Ceferino's ulterior motives were clear. He continued to take part in public life, the life he had fought to make his.

Sometimes, at those parties that were so very *sui generis*, he would touch José's balls, stroking him while, at the same time, with his tongue out, he would give Marta — José's wife — and Catalina a good going over. Later, convinced of his worldliness, he would snuggle up to his wife in bed and sleep like a baby, proud of his exploits at the evening's pathetic party. Don Ceferino had another name for "his friends". At this point in his life, for them — his fellow party-goers — he was the "little lizard" or the "old man". Filled with resentment for having put up with the slobbering fool and getting nothing positive out of it, economically speaking, that is what they called him. "Tomorrow I have to go to Madrid for the boring national budget", Don Ceferino told Marta, as he slid his tongue down her neck. "It is always a bore, but tomorrow after breakfast things are going to change."

SIX: ANOTHER CRANK OF THE LEVER, OR INTERESTS ALWAYS VESTED

Jordi Stalellas was a born politician. A good Catalan, from his mountaineering youth, seriousness had been his motto: seriousness in terms of fatherland and... of money. He married quite young; Mercedes was a young Catalan of the middle bourgeoisie, perfect as a support for all his ideals, especially the political ones. They would soon see their home made happy by the arrival of numerous healthy children. When the dictator was in his prime, Jordi had been held prisoner— like many other — due to some retreats held by Catalan independence supporters at the Capuchin monastery in Barcelona and another in Montserrat. This fact was going to serve as a medal, another honour, for Jordi's future career as a politician that would surprise many. Not him, of course, as his secret ambition had always driven him, from the beginning. And, although it took him many years to choose the path he would follow, this was for a reason. It was power, money and politics. Life and events led him to choose the second which, in turn, would lead him to the highest position in Catalonia, the presidency of the regional government.

Years later, and for different reasons and motives, his career would end in a manner similar to Ceferinito's, which had begun some years previous to his own. But, turning the crank in a quarter-turn backwards, we find ourselves with Jordi Stalellas, comfortably installed in the bourgeoisie of Barcelona, with a mate chosen with restraint, progressive, careful to have just the right tone in actions and manners. As I mentioned earlier, they are now the parents of a number of children. He is employed as the president of Montaña Bank, an up-and-coming organisation with even greater ambition in terms of Catalan ideals of love of country, highlighting its Catalan roots. Some time later, however, the bank (or Catalan association) — whose policy stated that only native-born Catalans who spoke the language perfectly could work there, even in jobs like cleaning lady or unpaid intern — filed for bankruptcy. Jordi knew how to exploit — or, better put — stir up the Catalans' feelings, talking to them about their roots in order to increase and multiply his number of investor accounts. But when the bank filed for bankruptcy and the scandal became public — what happened? why? when? — it was like one of those hurricanes that you know is coming, but that you think is never really going to happen, although it does eventually turn up, ruthlessly laying waste to homes, cars and people. The bank's hurricane also laid waste, true, but most especially to the accounts of small investors who could never have imagined or — as commonly said —"seen it coming". However, this is where Jordi's true career was going to have a touchstone, a reference, a relationship, a concordance with him, with the other piece of this chess game, a piece related to Jordi, the former bank president and future president. But... let us not put the cart before the horse, because it is now, at this precise moment, that another important piece in the game appears on stage. In other words, Don Ceferino, the ex-Ceferinito from his hometown Martos.

SEVEN: THE COVERT

In bullfighting, the covert is the barrier behind which the bullfighter stands to escape the beast when he gets dangerously close. The bullfighter is used to simply leaping over the barrier and saving himself from being gored by the raging bull threatening to kill him.

Late that morning, Don Ceferino ate his breakfast quickly. He did not even drink the orange juice that Montserrat always had the maid leave him on the dining room table. He greeted the doorman and crossed the promenade to catch a taxi on the Diagonal, but Don Ceferino was worried. The Socialists were putting on the squeeze; members of Esquerra were demanding explanations and he could go on no more. It was not advisable to be at the front to judge Jordi once he had been seated as president. Many long-closed boxes had been opened and, rather than smell, they stank. But one thing made him sketch a smile as he arrived at court; taking the decision to retire a year earlier. It was the right thing to do.

EIGHT: THE TRICK

I decided to investigate. I decided to get some information on the property in Calvia near the hotel where Tania and I stayed. I decided to take the first step and ask. I had met him at an exhibition, in a hall on Layetana Street, where we had spoken very briefly, but he had given me his business card. I looked in that box where I kept all the business cards, postcards and newspaper clippings that I always planned to read later. And there it was: Ceferino Dominguez del Ciervo, lawyer, President of the General Council of the Judiciary. I rang the number he had marked at the bottom right and, coincidentally, he himself answered my call. A cheerful voice. Yes, yes, he remembered; yes, I could stop by and see him in the morning. Tomorrow at noon, I wrote down, along with the address, which was not the one on the card. My wristwatch said it was twelve o'clock sharp when I rang the bell at the door of a flat located on the left side of the Eixample. It was Don Ceferino in person who opened the door; he had the air conditioning on and I was surprised to see him in shirtsleeves. His smile invited me to come in. His hand escaped him, flying and sliding slimily, while he simultaneously smiled at me, confused. I admired some paintings and some nice pieces of indisputable good taste, while he accompanied me to the centre area; the house was far more like a flat than an office. We sat on a chair made in a quite ridiculous French style, in contrast to the rest of the decoration (Ceferino was president of the association of art critics), and there were certainly no more words with his hands. He began to walk back and forth; I was confused, dazed and terribly embarrassed for him, as he babbled. Don Ceferino, however, had opened his fly, and I could glimpse some flamboyant bubblegum pink boxers. I think I recall that they had some kind of little green frogs repeated several times, but not many, making him look completely ridiculous. I was carrying a dossier on the Nazi matter that I wanted to show him, but, speaking in legal terms, there was no place and no time. With strength that was unusual for his 75 years, he grabbed me, pushed my face against his penis... Without another thought, I grabbed by bag and, hitting him in the back of the neck with it, I got out of there, running down the stairs instead of waiting for the lift, feeling like I had been completely taken in. once again, life had played me and this time with someone who was supposedly respectable. Outdoors, I was able to take a deep breath and I began to walk in an effort to calm myself.

NINE: THE STRENGTH OF THE INTEREST

The cards had been dealt and well played. Jordi Stalellas had handled them with a skill worthy of the finest illusionist. The accusations, the new president's prosecutor, the news in the press and on TV... he had been able to skilfully spin them in his favour. He had managed to turn himself into the scapegoat of the government in Madrid. Like a miracle, and like in a game of darts where those throwing them manage to use a fantastic magnet to turn them towards the aggressor, Jordi had leveraged the right moment to turn himself into a martyr for everything that contradicted his morality. And what a miracle, indeed! For he had been smart enough to swim the turbid waters without muddying himself, emerging more spotless than ever, if possible. Even the general public was unaware of what had happened, or the how or the why of it, or even the how much... most especially, I must say, the how much. Everything was already smoothly back on track, running its course in silence and, magically, it was not mentioned again on the news on television.

As for me, I still had to put up with Don Ceferino propositioning me in order to get my matters taken care of. He proposed we take part in group lovemaking. "You have a married girlfriend who might want to do it?" he actually asked me. Another day, when I was brave enough bring up the subject of Mallorca again, he told me, "I had a girlfriend who did it with her husband, but she died from drugs". And I was thinking, "from the disgust she felt from putting up with you, the poor thing". Meanwhile, the issue of the Nazis and the proof remained just that, proof and all I was left with was the certainty that, back on Mallorca, the house, the property and perhaps the group of pro-Nazi Hess followers would continue as before. I was entirely clueless as to why and what for. Meanwhile, giving another crank of the lever, I am writing this tale, these pages, like fragments of memories that — the stuff of imagination? dreams? — are already yesterday.

FORGET DORMANS

It was decided: Sarah would spend the school year in France. When I went to investigate boarding school arrangements in the French secondary school, the woman with perky breasts who had received me in her office without pronouncing hardly a word handed me the brochure advertising Inter-Europe, the boarding school for boys and girls that offered tennis, surfing, horseback riding... and whose photos were filled with smiling children doing it, filling classes where teachers pointed their pencils at maps, everyone smiling happily. There were also photos of the canteens, lounges and lovely, well-tended park surrounding the former hotel and spa, now a school. Back home, in the taxi, I thumbed through the brochure that accompanied the information pamphlet, looking at the prices. Damn! I was going to win the lottery in order to pay for Sarah's school. The prices were three times what I was paying in the Catholic school she attended in Barcelona. She had started going there when my divorce was finalised, partially due to inertia and mostly due to the lack of financial means. She continued going there for five years. I am thoroughly convinced that it is important to take your children to a school that shares as much as possible the ethical and moral knowledge you use to deal with life. Because, if you do not, there comes a time — when children see things more clearly — in which a divergence with you takes place if you deal with life in a way that totally contradicts the norms that they see the faculty, students and parents at their school using to guide their own lives. This is basic. In some respects, my way of dealing with life does not seem to mesh with the norms that govern or prevail over the Jesuit priests and some of the parents who take their children there.

When the taxi dropped me off at home, I had already decided to not take a holiday that summer. In August, Sarah would visit her father, as she did every year. And I would have a chance to save by staying in Barcelona. I would rest, get a little bored after a year of tense work and the battle of living paycheck to paycheck when I had overspent. This is quite easy to do when you take into account my meagre fixed salary and the seasons when I had to buy a new bag, jeans — but designer ones — for Sarah, who seemed to be growing taller month by month. She was growing so much that everything was too small or too short.

Well, now I was going to save and try to have Sarah study for a whole school year in Champagne. So then she could continue studying the following year in the French secondary school and talk to me in my language, since she did not learn it before or after the divorce. Her father talked to me in Catalan so as to not disturb his mother, who lived with us and felt left out if we spoke in French. With her around — and she was always around — we gradually stopped speaking it.

I had just collected my commission as manager in a contract between a French singer and company that made dairy products (yogurt, milk, cookies, everything dietetic) for their adverts, and I decided to keep the money in a separate account for Sarah's school. I spoke with Dormans, with the school, several times, getting information on the curriculum what clothes she should wear (everything had to be marked with her name). I sent a cheque as a deposit to reserve a place for her and got ready to fill in the various forms they sent me together with the receipt for the money. Health certificate, diseases that the girl had had since birth, photocopies, forms which had the most diverse questions: do you allow your daughter to smoke? A twelve-year-old girl? Can she go out alone? Did she have a correspondence in Dormans?

So, the departure day arrived. Since we would have needed a servant to help us with the bags, I decided to have them shipped.

I had marked her sheets, all her clothing, etc., as instructed in the information pamphlet they had sent me with the paperwork.

The Sants station was full of people. Most were tourists returning to their respective countries after finishing their holidays. Many, with their backpacks completely covering their backs; others, with souvenirs. The air was filled with the usual end-of-summer-holiday vibe. We descended on the escalator to the basement, where the trains departing to Paris are located. First, some ladies with their black suits and wicker suitcases tied with old belts; then, a group of fans of who-knows-what team. Gradually, the platform filled with a motley group of chattering people. The uniformed man in a navy blue cap tells us which car is ours and that, as expected, the train to Paris is expected to leave at the scheduled time.

We settled into our compartment and checked that, indeed, we had the bed number on the ticket and, almost without us realising it, the train started. The city was already behind us and quickly entered polluted fields with empty plastic detergent or oil bottles scattered among the bush. I closed the curtain, and after eating a couple of sandwiches we had bought in the café, Sarah and I got ready to sleep. A hazy cloud flooded my mind and I fell asleep quickly.

The man in the blue cap knocked on our door at 7:30 am. We were going to arrive in Paris in half an hour. We had just enough time to dress and wash up a little; we finished breakfast in the café, when the train entered the main station.

With a piece of luggage in each hand, Sarah and I descend to the platform. The air was colder and contrasted with Barcelona's thick and humid air the previous day. We queued to wait for a taxi to take us to the Gare de l'Est, where we picked up our ticket to Dormans in Marne, but it did not leave until 2:15 pm, so we had four hours to wait.

We looked at the shop windows in the station, bought a couple of camembert sandwiches in the brasserie and ordered coffee with milk.

We sat down in a corner next to the mirrors. The brasserie was almost full. We put our jackets aside on the soft maroon bench and waited. Sarah asked me for a franc for the door of the toilet and then I went myself. I had read the newspaper and the *Jours de France* nearly from start to finish. Although it seemed impossible, 2:15 finally arrived and our train's number and track was showing on the display. Sarah quickly bought another camembert sandwich in the kiosk and I bought some pasta and we rushed to get on the train, which left right on schedule.

It was a modern train and all the cars were the same. They had modern comfortable tangerine-coloured seats with folding tables where we played cards. The train was almost empty; only three or four people were scattered among the seats closest to the windows.

We had been travelling for fifteen minutes when I noticed a man with white hair and a moustache who was travelling in front of us. He was very elegant, wearing a navy blue suit, white shirt and maroon tie. Apparently, he wanted to talk, because he used a trivial excuse to engage in conversation with us or — better put — me, since Sarah was still playing cards, very interested in the Gin Rummy I had just taught her. The man was from Château-Thierry (the homeland of fable collector La Fontaine). He had recently retired, apparently from a mid-to-high-level position, based on his clothing. After discovering from me that I came from Spain, he politely asked what brought us to the area. "We are going to Dormans." "Yes, it is twenty-five kilometres from Château-Thierry. You should get ready and have your luggage neck to the door; the train stops just for a minute." He pointed out which door opened on the platform. "And why are you coming to Dormans?" "Oh, my daughter Sarah is going to study at Inter-Europe." His face changed imperceptibly, but it did change; I noticed. I attributed this to the adversity that apparently existed between the inhabitants of Château-Thierry and of Dormans which, in an apparently inexhaustible torrent of words, he had explained to me. But his destination was approaching and he got ready to get off the train, as it stopped just for a minute in Château-Thierry as well. He quickly said good-bye and got off.

We were practically alone in the car and we settled into the seats next to the exit door. The quarter-hour separating one town from the other passed quickly, and we already were at the door ready to get off at the next stop. I felt something cold in my stomach. I was going to leave Sarah here for a long year, in a place unknown to us but that now, in a few minutes, we were going to get to know.

We made a mistake and got off on the opposite side, so we were on the ground. The train passed quickly and we crossed the track. Our car was close to the front, so we had to walk a bit to get to the little station.

There were other people walking quickly; they crossed the small room and got into their cars parked outside.

In front of us was a smiling young man about twenty-five years old; he was dark, tall, had curly hair, black eyes, was not bad looking and wore an ironic smile. After asking us, he took our bags and we went with him to a white van near the entrance. Sarah and I sat in the back and he got behind the wheel.

He looked at me in the rearview mirror. The kid was not French. Mixed race: yes. African: perhaps. A former student who had likely lost his parents and stayed on as a chauffeur or handyman at the school, I assumed. He drove quickly and the countryside was pretty. Without realising it, we passed through the white gates of Inter-Europe and then we were on the steps before the elegant front door. We went in and, in the huge lobby with oriental rugs, a man past his forties came towards us. He was tall, had greyish hair, blue eyes behind a pair of glasses that were modern but discreet, and was correctly dressed in a suit and tie. He kindly invited us to go into the next room, which was a huge office. There were two Louis XVI style desks, and an impressive Boule clock over the stone fireplace. A woman of about his age, with short auburn hair, slight embonpoint which she sought to hide with her completely black suit and elegant mid-heeled shoes, was close to one of the desks and smiled at me without shaking my hand.

Sarah and I saw down on two armchairs, and the director, Mr Joannet — as he had introduced himself — sat down behind his desk. As I was seated and looked at him, I noticed his eyes were very light-coloured and his smile seemed sadistic. I thought perhaps he wanted to give himself a cosmopolitan air, living as he was in a village, and did not give it more importance. He looked at me across his desk, smiling; I also noticed the attention the woman in black was paying me. I figured it was time to pay (I already had sent some money from Barcelona to reserve a place). Now it was time to pay for September. I pulled out the chequebook and got ready to write a cheque for a considerable amount. Mr Joannet clarified to me that, since it was almost the middle of the month, it would be slightly less. Good. He handed me the receipt and asked me for Sarah's passport, which was needed for her to go to Switzerland, where they would spend 15 days skiing in March. My daughter elbowed me, telling me in Spanish that she did not want to go skiing (we had spent a Christmas holiday in the snow and she was not enthusiastic about skiing).

"Mr Joannet, can Sarah skip the skiing?" "Oh, she will want to go," he answered me with an even broader fake smile. I handed over the documents they had requested by mail: health certificate, study certificate, local government certificate, with generally quite good marks, and I was able to hold onto her national ID card as I said they would not need it for anything.

"With regard to religious education, what religion does your daughter belong to?" "Oh, she is Catholic, but we do not practise much," I answered. He smiled and stood, ending the interview. The woman in black, a bit further away to my right, also stood. Mr Joannet accompanied us to the door telling me that for the holidays, they would take care of getting her to Paris so I would not have to trouble myself coming to Dormans. "We will talk," I answered.

"Is there a hotel in the town, please?" I enquired. "You know, so Sarah does not feel homesick, I am going to stick around for a few days and at the same time I will wait for the luggage to arrive." The director had told me in his office that he had already received the papers from the Paris to fill in and that they would arrive in a day or two. We went out and he quickly got behind the wheel of the long white van and passed in front of a small house. He got out with us and opened the door. There was a bar like the thousands you find in French villages. Behind the counter was a young man and four or five locals. Without further ado, he left us there. It was then when I had the impression that, after leaving the school, we — my daughter and I —were being watched by a number of eyes, including those of the gardener who was wearing white sweatpants, the kind for jogging, and had an idiotic expression on his classic "gorilla" face.

Without asking for our documents, the man at the bar accompanied us to a room facing the road. It had a double bed that had seen better times and a wash basin. Across the road was a sign that said: "Paris, 110 km". It was an old house, with a wooden floor that creaked quite a bit. Sarah and I washed up quickly and went downstairs to eat. Interestingly, given the extremely cheap price for full board, the food was very good. I found out later that the cook, who was twenty-seven, was the brother of Mr Mains, the owner, who had taken over running the hotel two months ago. The kid was an artist in the kitchen and in Barcelona he would have made a fortune with a little restaurant. The older servant was a hard-working woman; the younger one followed along, but at a slower pace. It was Sunday and there was entertainment. A long table full of members of a local family celebrating the birthday of a boy who looked to be about eight. There was joy in the dining room. Sarah made short work of her meal. She had chosen the cheapest one — though very well made — with an eye to sticking to our budget. I had given the owner my purse with francs and pesetas so that I would not be "wearing" my money everywhere I went.

It was very cold and damp. Unlike the humid heat we had left behind the previous day in Barcelona, it was quite noticeable.

After lunch and a coffee in the bar — apparently frequented by townspeople, where the black-and-white television and checkerboard for who-knows-what game were the main entertainment for the locals. That is, leaving aside the Pernod and Petit Blanc that came and went (the cold and the lack of other attractions seemed to be the reason that both men and women drank in Dormans). Three strangers came in; they seemed to know the place well. I guessed they were father, mother and daughter. The last seemed rather old and about six months pregnant. It looked like they had not brushed their hair in a month and wore what looked to be dirty borrowed clothes and trainers. They glanced at me suspiciously and took the corner table. There was a guest in the hotel whose appearance and attitude made him seem strange. He might have been Arab, but I could not say for sure. He was on the young side, wore out-of-style — but clean — clothing (sixties-style wide trousers, a mini sweater from '68), frizzy hair and a nasty face. He also ate lunch and dinner alone, and during daytime (I later noticed) he walked tirelessly back and forth across the town. When we ran into him in the dining room, he would great us with a nod of his head. Despite the greeting, the man was extremely vulgar.

We took a walk around Dormans. The town was one long street, high street, the road connecting Paris with Epernay and then Reims. In the middle of town was the church with a bell tower; it had a lovely clock. You could see the main shops along that long street: several nice-looking beauty salons, boutiques, a library, a butcher, several cafés, and even a modern shop with some good-looking readymade food. A little ways beyond the church was a big square where the Poste Credito Agricol was located, a pastry shop, telephones and the BNP (which has a branch in any town with more than 1,000 inhabitants) all converged. The square was big and served as a car park for many cars, but not that Sunday; it was deserted. Sarah and I walked, finding out where things were: the baker, winter shoes, stationery stores with things schoolgirls needed. All the shops announced that it was time to back to school.

We had dinner and slept soon, because the next morning we had to get up early. We asked to be woken up at seven o'clock with breakfast. They looked at us with surprise (later, I realised that taking a breakfast tray to the room was a luxury they were not used to or knew about at the Zumino Hotel). The room was like a cooler; the damp went through your skin right to your bones. We clung together under the sheet and the unsympathetic blanket. I put our jackets on top for a little extra warmth and we fell asleep holding onto each other, exhausted.

The girl, the slow one, knocked on the door at seven sharp. With half-closed eyes, I got up to open the door and she came in with the big breakfast tray. I did not give her a tip, but I did thank her. We jumped out of bed to brush our teeth and got dressed quickly. We continued to shiver. We were fast and in fifteen minutes we were going down the stairs leading to the bar. I soon realised that I did not recall whether the school was to the left or to the right of the hotel. I asked Mr Mains, who was already behind the bar, serving drinks to the locals, who were already numerous by now. He put on a leather jacket, guided us to the door where his car was and took us there himself. We entered the school's huge, well-tended park and he took us right to the door. I thanked him and got out with Sarah. He tried to ring the bell, but I saw that the door was open and gave it a push. We are in Inter-Europe's lobby. Hanging on the wall in front of us is the largest elephant tusk I have ever seen.

Three or four children of colour from six to thirteen years old are wandering about there. To the right, framed by the library, a big TV is turned on and showing the morning news. I ask a child where the teacher is and, since he does not know, I go to the room on the right where there are several tables prepared for breakfast. At the back, there is a stone fireplace; over it, the head of a big deer presides over the room.

A teacher finally appears. He is tall, strong, with the air of a sportsman. He has fairly short, brown hair, blue eyes, is suntanned and has the fine wrinkles of someone used to being outdoors; he looks nice. I recognise him as the one whose picture is in the information leaflet with several students queued up and ready to run down a slope. He takes charge of Sarah. I agree to pick her up at five and retrace the path I came on. I go through the lobby, close the door, walk through the garden. I run into the gardener in the white sweatpants. It is dirty, as if he had rolled around in the garden; he greets me with an idiotic smile; it is a stupid smile. I got out to the road and take the road to the left to walk back to the town.

After walking ten minutes along a big avenue full of dry leaves, which is also the road, I am already almost at the big square. I see a nice-looking café and go inside. The owner looks at me curiously.

There are three or four people in the bar drinking everlasting Pernord or white wine. I order a *café crème* and sit down at a table near the pool tables. There is a window in the ceiling through which a sunbeam passes and hits the green plants attractively hung, cheering up the room in general. The people at the bar are murmuring about something; my guess is that it is about me.

After leafing through the newspaper, I head to the phones to call the agency in Paris about the luggage. Sitting in the small telephone box in the Poste building, I find out from talking to Mr Boiteux that the papers to be filled in had reached the school days ago, but not yet been returned signed. "Yes, ma'am, we just need one signature, which confirms that the clothes contained in the suitcase is for an Inter-Europe student." "No, ma'am, no reply has been received, although someone did speak with the school's director, Mr Joannet, and he confirmed that he had received the papers. Yes, this happened more than a week ago, about ten days; there has been more than enough time to have received it."

I agreed that I would press the school and I exit the Poste building. Just then, the natural sunlight becomes hidden and a cold wind blows through the town.

While walking, I find myself in front of the bakery we saw yesterday. It is open and a pleasant smell of just-baked bread comes out. Tempted, I go inside to buy the chocolate-filled croissants Sarah likes so much. The baker is a tall, bald man with clean skin and a frank look.

"Are you in Dormans for work?", he asks me while I look for change in my big bag which is, in turn, full of little bags. It is hard to find the little change purse made of leather squares by touch. "Oh, no. My daughter is going to study here, at Inter-Europe." He gives me a surprised look and, for a moment, he seemed inhibited. He quickly recovers and returns the change along with the receipt with the price of the croissants. I thank him and exit the bakery without realising that the women in the queue have fallen silent for a moment and are observing me with curiosity. I walk along the high street; there are several beauty salons. I go into the stationary shop to buy the newspaper and then continue on to the hotel, where Mr Mais is still at the bar serving drinks and chatting with the locals who — except one or two — are the same ones as yesterday.

I have to call my mum. I ask for the phone hidden behind the bar and dial the prefixes for Spain and Barcelona. Mum's voice sounds cheerful when she picks up the phone. I tell her where we are and the hotel's phone number, and that I am going to stay on to settle the luggage issue. She says she is going to call me every night. It is better like that, for I am short on francs and calls from the hotel are expensive. Mr Mains has taken out a little calculator and the two minutes I spent calling Spain cost me a fortune.

A couple sitting near us in the dining room smile at us pleasantly. Both of them are nice and, interestingly, both are stained with paint; they must be painters, but not of landscapes. Despite their paint stains, they are modern, stylish and very attractive.

The day passes quickly and at five o'clock on the dot, I push open the big white door, which remains open. One of the little boys of colour from the morning is roaming around and I ask him about Sarah. Smiling, he takes me up some stairs towards one of the pavilions, the one on the right. She is in a large, spacious classroom talking with two friends. The fat boy is her age, more or less. He says he was born in Canada, but that his parents live in the Republic of Omar and work at the Petroleum Exchange. Yes, they are near Saudi Arabia, so he — Patrick — can only go to see them at Christmas. The other kid is Ali, around 14. He is slender, dark brown and elegant with a shifty, reserved look.

Through the window I see two boys playing ping-pong. One of them catches my eye, as he has an almost effeminate beauty. He is wearing very short shorts and a sleeveless t-shirt with the bottom carefully rolled up. In the distance, the Marne flows slowly among the beautiful forest. I sit at a desk and start to chat with Patrick, since the kid from Mali does not open his mouth. Suddenly, the hallway door opens and the teacher comes in. With a reproving look, he indicates to Patrick that they have to go to another room. I feel like a schoolgirl caught doing something wrong and I go down the stairs quickly with Sarah and exit the school. On the ground floor, two waitresses have started to set up long tables for dinner. On the road, we run into the gardener. He grins at me like a moron and is accompanied by an extraordinary young man of colour, dressed in elegant white pants and long tunic. When he sees us, he comes over to say hello to Sarah. It is logical to deduce that he knows her.

Sarah is happy. She shows me the pretty notebooks she had been given, a little bag with all kinds of pens and pencils, scissors and glue. She is determined to stay and oozes satisfaction. She tells me endlessly about her new friends. Especially about Alexandre. He is a 12-year-old French boy who is quite good-looking. "You saw him through the window playing ping-pong. Remember, mum?"

We walk around the town, but a light rain begins to fall so we head quickly over to the hotel. It is packed with people. September is not over yet and people are still going on holiday, plus the usual locals. When we enter the dining room, there is only one empty table left: ours.

We dine deliciously well. Then, a bit of TV and a game of dice in the lobby-bar that is still full of customers and then to sleep. When we get undressed, we practically jump into the damp sheets and try to warm each other up. I fall asleep lulled by the sound of the tyres of cars along the road going or coming to Paris or Reims, and perhaps of some truck whose driver, perhaps somewhat sleepy, gets distracted and has to slam on the brakes.

When the bell tower of the church next to square rings at eight o'clock, Sarah and I are wrapped in our jean jackets and walking towards the school. We are the only ones. Some children carrying their book-bags on their shoulders follow us, but go into the *l'école normale pour garçons* located just a few metres beyond the church.

We go into the school. Patrick, the idiot gardener, is wandering around. The big colour TV is on: a Parisian hairdresser is doing a demo of how to cut hair "Some coffee?" the tall and sporty teacher asks me. "Oh, no, I already had breakfast at the hotel, thank you."

A child of colour comes and goes. Today I will go to Paris to change my plane ticket to a week later. I decided that yesterday, as I was hugging Sarah in bed; there is something that is still preventing me from leaving her.

I checked, and there is a train leaving at ten, so, when I say goodbye to Sarah, I head to the train station, pick up my return ticket and go to the café across the street to have some coffee.

Unsurprisingly, there are locals already enjoying their endless Pernods or white wines. There are two pool tables, a juke box, a ski toilet and — in the back —a kitchen with the house; the woman appears every so often. The boss is a clone of Yves Montand — younger, but uglier —and it is immediately clear that, despite his macho vibe, it is his wife Domine who wears the pants. The girl — eight or nine years old — is also there; she must also go to *l'école normale pour jeunes filles*. The customers stare at me from the corners of their eyes; they must be wondering who I am. They will soon find out. The boss talks about the train schedule. "Yes, they run on time (he had already figured it out)." "Do you work here?" "No. I have a daughter studying at Inter-Europe." Was it my imagination or did it seem to me that the conversation stopped and a second of silence fell on the station bar?

I paid and I went to the little station across the street to look at leaflets and wait for my train. It finally arrived, on time, and I arrived in Gare de L'est within an hour. When I got off onto the platform, I no longer felt lost. I turned towards the exit. As I was hungry and did not want to spend much money, I bought a camembert sandwich at the kiosk. Eating it, I walked towards an exit door where there was a taxi rank, but there were none.And when one did appear, the driver seemed to not see me. Finally, one rolled down his window and told me that no one would pick me up until I finished my sandwich. The hell with that! I went back inside the *gare* and strolled about, eating slowly. I note that there is a subway and, underneath, a travel agency. I go in and queue up. The woman would win no prizes for her attitude, but finally, after paying for the service, I managed to change the plane ticket to a week later.

When leaving, I stop into a café opposite after browsing a stand with different colours of hair gel, natural products, African jewellery and so on. Mum would call it junk, but I love it.

I buy newspapers and try to pass the time until five, when the train to Dormans leaves. The trip passes quickly among groups of people returning to their homes after work. The Paris suburb has a very particular vibe; that afternoon, it makes me recall Buffet's grey and somewhat gloomy etchings, with the monotonous, unique buildings; to me, they are beautiful. I get off quickly in Dormans with 30 other people also getting off. At the station's exit are two or three taxis and several parked cars that quickly start to move. I choose to not take any and I start up the slightly steep path that will carry me to the curve and then to the road, the high street that leads to the school. I pass by the stationary shop and the bakery and quicken my pace, for it is already past six (that morning, when I saw the return time for the Paris-Dormans train, I took the precaution of calling Mr Joannet from the bar of the *gare* so he would tell Sarah that her mum would be picking her up late). Anyway, I pick up my pace and run into Patrick coming out of the bakery a bit further away. He is wearing the same, increasingly filthy, white sweatpants and his mouth and face were also dirty. He smiles at me maliciously. Good God, what a freak! Now I am entering Inter-Europe. Sarah was waiting for me. She is cheerful, happy; she shows me her homework. She has so many things to tell me... Amicably, I retrace my path, but with her. We take the words right out of each others' mouths talking about the day's developments and we are getting close to the *gare* where Mr "Yves Montand" is serving paella, the day's specialty. Sarah orders two camembert sandwiches and right there I help her to do her homework.

She tries to play a record in the *juke box* (she had never seen one), but we are unsuccessful; "Yves Montand" helps us. Now it is playing; it sounds great. We do it again. The wife comes out; the one who actually wears the pants.

I notice that her hair is nicely cut and ask her about her hairdresser. "OK, yes, ma'am, I'm a foreigner", "I have seen several. Which one is best?". As I imagined, she is the typical "bossy dictator" and is delighted to tell me where they really cut hair well. "But, you know, for your daughter, it is not worth it." Before, she had heard from her husband that she was going to stay at Inter-Europe. "Oh, Joel (the professor with the explorer look that wanders around the school) often comes here for a drink; yes, we know him well." The people of this town are definitely not given to talking much; that is not their sin. Okay, but for those "not in the know", there is certainly something that could be said. We pay for what we had and head over to the hotel. It is a short and pleasant walk and autumn is falling softly on Dormans.

The regulars are in the hotel; France is definitely not a nation of teetotallers. After peeing, I stand up on the old toilet seat and, through the dormer window, I see the rooftops of the upper part of town, very near the cemetery, and a lot of peace and tranquillity in the air. I wash and we go downstairs to dinner. Sarah plays with the son of the couple who own the hotel. His name is Romual; he is two and a half and loves his new little friend. Sarah puts together a little toy car that came inside a chocolate egg I bought him at the bakery and he plays happily.

"Do not make work for them", the older servant says to him. Because she takes so much care with her job and attending to the customers, she is like a member of the family. "Oh! No need to worry. We love kids", I answer her. Sarah, as always, makes short work of the cheese plate and we go with Romuald to the bar-lounge-hall of the Zumiro Hotel.

Madame Mais, a young, thin and pleasant-looking woman, began conversing with me. She should have gone to Spain this summer, yes, to Ampuriabrava but, ultimately, it did not work out, as they had taken over the hotel and had to work.

The conversation went on, talking about children. I feel like the woman likes me; she tells me about Inter-Europe. "Did you know? Two or three years ago it burned down completely. They even had to close it, as it was almost totally destroyed (I remembered that the dormitory pavilions had been recently built). The children of an African president were here; he came to pick them up with a helicopter. It was on television; I remember that I was living in Epernay then and I saw it. There was also an article in *Paris Match*.

Some said that one of the kids had fallen asleep smoking, but the townspeople said that someone burned it, that it was the revenge of a father." A cold shiver ran down my back, but I remained seated on the stool and speaking calmly, as if nothing had happened. Meanwhile, Sarah was playing with Romuald and his little toy car. The senior maid would tell me the next day, while she was serving me lunch — after I mentioned the horror of the burnt school and the two children who died that night — that she had served the parents of the two dead children. "Yes, at that table right next to this one. Oh, ma'am, they were devastated, poor people."

That night, in our cold double bed, while my daughter is asleep, the images flash through my mind. The school in flames. Me, visiting the dormitory pavilion. We had a right to choose her bed as not all of the students had come yet. We chose — after looking at two other beds— one that was close to the radiator for her feet and away from the window. The lady (one of them, because there were two), who accompanied us at the request of Mr Joannet checked to see whether the bed was made. "No, no sheets; you can have it." I saw that it had a small sink, a shower and not a single cupboard. "Ah, the cupboards are downstairs." I had no opportunity to see them. Later, I found out from Sarah that they were in the basement. The "cupboards" were one big cupboard with a sliding door that held the boarders' clothing. At least, that is how my daughter explained it to me.

The next day, as was usual, I accompanied Sarah to school. The bell was ringing eight o'clock when the two of us, wrapped up in our jean jackets, were racing towards the school. As always, the TV is on in the entryway *lobby*. Guy — as the teacher in the ski photos is called — offers me a coffee, which I gently refuse.

After dropping off my daughter, I head to the station and pick up a ticket for Reims. I need to go to Courlancy to pay a visit. The train passes through the Marne valley with its impressive Soissons Castle like something out of a fairy tale, and I soon stop in Reims. The station is quite big and, when I leave the platform, I head over to a taxi that takes me to the big hospital in Courlancy. In the hubbub of people, I take some time to find the office, but I am finally received by the secretary of Dr Lamarque, who gives me a brochure with the lab tests needed before he ties my tubes. I find out what the price is; it is considerably cheaper than in Spain, so I consider the possibility of having it done here. When I leave, the sun is shining nicely and it is almost hot. Unlike Dormans', Reims's weather is always warmer and less damp. I walk to the bus stop that drops me off in Cathedral Square. The cathedral looks majestic on this autumn evening, golden and warm. The streets are bustling with people walking to and fro.

I catch another bus and it takes me to the *gare*. I wait for my train back to Dormans.

It is almost dark when I pass through Inter-Europe's gate. Patrick frightens me, because I suddenly run into him in front of me, with his everlasting stupid smile and filthy white sweatpants, as if he had just wallowed in the mud. I greet him pleasantly and pick up Sarah, who is happy and full of things to tell me. We head to the stationery shop on the way to the hotel way to buy a dictionary and some writing supplies. The woman looks at me puzzled when I tell her that my daughter goes to the school, or am I imagining things? I do not give it another thought and we go to the hotel for dinner, for we are starving. Before, at the school, while waiting to Sarah, I went through a room decorated in a decidedly rococo style. Joel — the one who looked like an explorer — has come to say hello to me; apparently he likes to visit the region. He said, "Oh, yes! I was in Reims today; the cathedral is beautiful", and we continued the conversation but changing the topic to Spain and its tourist scenery which Joel seems to know quite well. Suddenly, Sarah entered and cuts off the conversation. I do not like the guy; there is definitely something weird about him.

The hotel dining room is packed with people. Our table is reserved for us and we make ourselves comfortable. Romualdo is not here today. We ask the senior maid about him. He is at home today. After dinner, when we get back to the room, we fall down exhausted. Tomorrow will be another day.

The next day, is a repetition of the everyday routine: breakfast, now in hall-bar-lounge and then quickly putting on our jackets and going out to walk to the school. The suitcases have not yet arrived, so, when I drop Sarah off, I am going to the phones to call the transport offices in Paris. The manager Mr Boiteux, tells me that they have now sent two letters to the school and have not yet received the signature. He cannot explain it, as two weeks have passed by now. I exit the office in the Poste and go next to Credit Agrícole, to change travellers' cheques, which I had bought in Barcelona just in case someone robbed us on the train, but that no one accepted in the town. At the counter, while doing the paperwork, the employee seems curious. "And how is it that you are not French and what are you doing around here?" I explain the usual, "I have an eleven-year-old daughter who is studying at Inter-Europe". What does it seem to me that his gaze suddenly turned cold? I give it no more thought and go to the hotel; the temperature has dropped and I order a nice hot *café crème*.

I find out how to get a taxi to Paris, because I have been thinking over the idea of going to collect the bags for days. As they are very heavy, I cannot bring them on the train and one of the locals — apparently a taxi driver — gives me a price. I tell him that I will think about it and I get ready to eat when the time comes. The nice painters show up soon afterwards and sit down two tables away. "Are you on holiday?" The idea makes me smile. That is just what I needed. Actually, this is the last place I would choose to spend a holiday, with so much cold. And that is what I tell them. They smile understandingly. I explain the usual, plus that I am from Barcelona. "Oh, Barcelona." The two have been there and they love it; Ibiza, too. They are really nice. They explain to me that they are painting some houses that store *champagne*. By the time I finish eating, I have already decided, I will call a phone number I wrote down coming from the school. It was on a car and it had the taxi and the phone next to it. Said and done. I phone from the bar; I have been given a price for a return trip plus a one-hour wait, and I give them my address. The voice answers that it is on its way here. Not ten minutes later, when I had just finished my coffee, a Citroën taxi stops on the road in front of the hotel. I go out. A man, about 30 years, opens the door and invites me to get in next to him. We leave for Paris.

The sun is shining directly on our knees and I appreciate the warmth after the dampness of the hotel. The road is pretty, nice. We go through Château-Thierry, homeland of La Fontaine and of the taxi driver, as he tells me proudly. I explain that I have to go to Pantin, on the outskirts, so it will not be necessary to cross the city.

The driver drives prudently, so there is some conversation. I once again explain the delay with the luggage and the reasons for my trip to Dormans. "My daughter is going to study at Inter-Europe." His conversation, until then fairly fluid, stops. There is a lapse of time while the road with its vineyards of Champagne grapes passes quickly. Puzzled, I ask him, "I think there is something strange about that school, is there not?" "Ma'am, there are some very strange things." "For example?", I continue digging. "They settle their problems among themselves; it is like an island in the middle of the town. When a child breaks a leg, or an arm (and you can imagine that, with an average of 120 kids, this does happen during a school year), they never call any of the town's ambulances. My wife has one. And they do not even go to any of the doctors in Dormans. They only one who treats them is an African doctor known for practicing black magic. Oh, and nobody from around here takes their children to that school, ever. They only accept boarding students, and they are usually the children of French citizens working in colonies or similar cases. It is strange, very strange."

We arrive in Pantin and I get out at a corner bar to ask the way to the offices from the transport agency. It was not hard to find them. The paperwork was not fast, but within an hour we were back in the car with the luggage and on our way back to Dormans. I decided to leave the luggage at the hotel. I had too many doubts in my head to decide to leave Sarah in a place that is starting to make me suspicious. After leaving luggage and paying the taxi driver, I head out to pick up Sarah. The cold feels very damp in Dormans. The school looks creepy in the shadows of the night as it falls, enveloping it quickly. Sarah is waiting for me, overjoyed. The day was fantastic.

As we were making our way on the road back, Patrick is coming on the road in front, filthy as always. In his hand is a bag with cakes which he is gradually eating. He is wearing his eternal stained white sweatpants and at his side is a slender elegant young dark-skinned man, impeccably dressed in white tunic and trousers. He crosses the road and says hello to Sarah. "Are you going tonight, too?" His eyes are bloodshot and his white smile glows against his ebony skin.

We continue our walk towards the hotel. "You know, mum?" Sarah says to me. "Camel, the kid you saw yesterday, has gone back to his country, Canada. At noon, while we ate, he came to say goodbye to us." Suddenly, I react. "I did not ask him why he was leaving. Oh, I do not know, we were eating, he did not have time, but I think he is with his parents here in a hotel." (We had seen that, right next to the Zumino Hotel, there is another, more luxurious one). "Well, as he is not in ours, he must be in the other one; I will go talk to his parents." After dinner, I put on my jacket and exit in direction of the other hotel. I go in and a kind and polite middle-aged woman walks over to me. "What would you like, ma'am?" "Oh, are you the owner? I was wondering whether there are some people here with a boy about fourteen, whether they are staying at this hotel." I show her a small black-and-white ID card photo of Camel that Sarah gave to me with his addresses in Canada and Dakar. "No, ma'am, they have not have been here. Feel free to look." Meanwhile, she approached her husband, who is wearing a chef's toque and is impeccably dressed in white. They must think I am frightened. "But you are Spanish. Who would have guessed, with such blonde hair and white skin! We know Spain well, we come often: Barcelona, Malaga, etc. It was precisely in Malaga that this portrait was done for my husband." She shows me a well-done oil painting in which he appears dressed as he is today, like a cook, but ten years younger. They are fans of Spain, that is clear, and good people. I ask about the school and their eyes change. In a quick moment, I tell them about my suspicions. They take me aside, away from the servants and the headwaiter. "You know, they always listen." The two look at each other, look at Sarah, who has joined me during this time. "Look, ma'am, we get a lot of customers here who take their kids to Inter-Europe. They do not ask us, we do not say anything; we do not want problems. You know? This is a small town; everybody knows each other. But, listen to what I say, ma'am; go back to Barcelona (his eyes are honest and look at me filled with tears). I have no grandchildren, but I would never take them to that place. It is not serious; I cannot tell you more. Strange things go on there: drugs, child prostitution. Flee, ma'am, you still have time; they are bad people, strange. Send your daughter to a French school in Barcelona and speak French to her at meals, but run from this hell." She has spoken. She is terrified. I hug her and take Sarah with me to the hotel. We take just what we need to change from the luggage for, after so many days wearing the same clothes, you appreciate something clean and some warm socks.While Sarah is sleeping, I come up with the plan of action for tomorrow. Through the window I see the sign that says "Paris, 110 km.", shrouded in fog, and return to bed to try to sleep so I will have all the strength I need the next day. In the morning, after spending almost the entire night awake, my plan is now meticulously designed. I have just put our stuff in the luggage and I close it. Sarah complains because she had class today and wants to keep on going to the school. We go down to breakfast in the bar-hall-lounge; from there, I call Inter-Europe and ask for Mr Joannet. At first, the voice answering the phone — I think it is Guy — says that he is not in, but a minute later, he changes his mind. "One moment, I will transfer you." "Mr Joannet, this is Madame Roldan. I am terribly sorry, but the embassy has informed me that Sarah's father is demanding she returns to Barcelona, so we must go back to Spain. I will come by in a taxi to pick up her passport in half an hour." Next, I call the taxi driver from the evening before and I ask for the bill so I can pay the hotel. It is pouring rain; through the streaming windows of the hotel, I see the taxi stop out front. We say good-bye to the owners and help to take out the bags and put them in the boot.

When we arrive in front of the hotel's gate, the taxi driver refuses to enter the park. Holding a small umbrella, I head towards the school. Sarah insists on coming with me. It is raining so intensely that it is hard for us to walk. Patrick opens the door for us, smiling moronically and says, "*Bonjour,* Cris". How does he know my name? I meet the clear, cold gaze of Mr Joannet. I accompany him to his luxurious office where he sits down behind his desk; I sit down in front. Sarah has decided to go up to the classrooms to say good-bye to her classmates.

As if by magic, I have bodyguards behind me. It is Guy and Joel; one on my left and another on my right. Mr Joannet waits for me to speak. I tell him about the news from the embassy, but in more detail. He has Sarah's school file ready; all he paperwork I had filled in when I brought her and her passport. The latter is what most interests me. He finally give it to me, without a question. I leave with Sarah; it is still raining cats and dogs. When she gets into the taxi, Sarah tells me she needs to return some homework that a classmate lent her yesterday to copy. I get angry and tell her to not bother. "Well, but quickly, okay?" The taxi driver is nervous. She leaves and I look at the clock. Five, ten, fifteen minutes go by and Sarah does not appear. "One more minute and I will go and get her", I tell Mr Roquet, for that is the taxi driver's name. Then Sarah appears, soaking wet. They had closed the doors and blocked them with chairs; she had had to jump.

We took off quickly towards Château-Thierry, where there is a travel agency. We need to change my ticket — to today, if possible — and charge the one for Sarah with my Visa. I am out of money and I still have to pay the taxi driver who has to return to the town after dropping us of in Orly. The woman at the agency is very nice. I vaguely explain the problem to her. She says she does not understand how the townspeople do not talk about what is going on in that school more clearly. I get the impression that she knows exactly what is going on. It no longer matters. When in doubt, a full retreat is better than leaving my eleven-year-old daughter there to find out. That is for sure. The woman tells me that the Visa machine is not working right, but that she will try to fix it to help me. She fiddles with it and it works on her second attempt. Well, we have confirmed tickets for today, Paris-Barcelona at 5:15. I smile happily, we say goodbye and we continue on our journey. We arrive without anything worthy of mention, say an affectionate good-bye to Mr Roquet and get ready to be patient in Orly.

Now on the plane on route to Barcelona, I can gently squeeze my daughter's hand, my mind at rest.

A MOROCCAN STORY

I opened the window to breathe; the Pacific air came in through it. The day was clear with a high, cloudless sky. The air brings me aromas of rose and jasmine, and all mixed with that distant sound of waves that come to die again and again on the sand. Yes, everything was beautiful, everything; I breathed the aroma of nature and life no, no, no... It was not Tangier.

Domingo was small and chubby, slightly obese. Every day, around 9 in the morning, leaving his house in his "full" navy blue suit, made of a shiny alpaca, as if it had been ironed and worn many times. He took Freedom Street to the big square, where the muezzin was beginning his prayer. He still had time to have his shoes cleaned by the urchin that worked as a shoeshine boy on the nearby corner. At the same time I — who was seven — was heading to the French school, wolfing down my bread with chocolate directly opposite Banco Espanyol, where the rather stiff teacher stood, usually holding an open notebook; and the same thing, on time, every day. Earlier, the *mousmé* had put my hair into two long braids. I always complained about how she pulled on my hair and she would grumble, "Girl, it is impossible to run a comb through your hair! Your aunt should take you to the salon for a good cut! That way, you would not be late to school again; your teacher, when I find her in the market..." And she continued on with her incessant, always different, chitchat. From my window, I could see the sea quite well; close and far away at the same time. I have loved it for years. At break time, I ate the cake that Fatima had prepared for me, on the playground, under a fig tree, looking vaguely at the sea, which constantly changed colour according to what time it was. I was a lonely, quiet child who spent hours absorbed in fantasy-filled dreams. "Wake up," Fatima said to me softly while we were returning home after leaving the school for the afternoon around five. The big square was packed with people who were buying and selling, and I liked to observe it: I became lost in thought watching how they haggled over the price of a blanket. The woman, standing, with her long caftan, and the Arab man, sitting, without losing his dignity. It was a never-ending lesson on civilization and culture, on colours and aromas, being offered up free-of-charge, in my view, in that square to a girl of my age, and who, aware of this, I tried to not let escape me. Oh, how would I feel homesick years later for this Africa that was leaving me so deeply marked.

The Dominguez family were Spaniards who had been living in Tangier ever since the father had been posted there by the bank some years before, before I was born. They lived in an apartment opposite ours. The family consisted of the father, mother and two kids a little older than me; they went to the school run by the Spanish parents. The mother, a small woman with a pot belly that she tried to hide by wearing floppy, loose black suits. Her hair was the colour of a fly's wings, and she liked to go all puffed up, as if she were going to take flight from one moment to another, very stiff and rigid. "Those people cannot talk without screaming", my aunt would say, opening the door when she came home from work, while leaving her leather bag on a small table at the entrance, under a Louis XV mirror. My aunt was going on thirty. Tall and distinguished, she had strawberry blonde hair which she wore in the style of Joan of Arc, very trendy at the time. With regular features, she had beautiful grey eyes, not too big, not too happy, but which — when laughing — filled with tiny bright green dots. Usually, my aunt got her clothes from the only French boutique in Tangier; they were quite classic, i.e. tailored suits or sport outfits, but always, always, skirts. She treated me with distant affection, like someone driven more by duty, or obligation, than by natural feelings.

Life for me took place in a private universe, personal only at the current time, in the small number of people around me and that did not have an excessively important role in the evolution of the Moroccan social life of that period. In Africa, things, facts take on totally different tone in Europe; I mean that the people who are born there, or who have been living there for a certain time have a certain dose of fatalism when it comes to existing. We do not frequent either the French colony or the Spanish one, not even the Polish one; we... we like a little island, alone, in the midst of such very different cultures. We belong to ourselves, and based on these coordinates, we acted.

At Christmas, the Dominguez got together on Christmas Eve, nicely dressed in their very best clothes, and sang songs in front of a manger installed in the dining room on a small wooden table. They put grass on it, brought by the *mousmée* from the closest field. They also played tambourines and Mrs Dominguez would get a little homesick, so little tears would slip out of her eyes while her husband would pat her on the back. I watched with curiosity, since they usually invited me to see the manger and to eat *turrón*, which my aunt called "nougat".

At home, that day was like any other. Only, some days before, my aunt had brought a bottle of French champagne that the three of us drank seated at the dining room table; I just wet my lips a bit. The summers come to my memory as a succession of blue and golden days, days of endless beaches of fine sand, cold water and a strong taste of salt. I usually went home when the sun went to bed. Then, my body felt tired, hurt, exhausted from so much air. And, when I got home, I would find Fatima complaining because the fried fish was cold and I would think, "and like cardboard". I would sit, alone, in the dining room and eat it without another word.

And so passed a year and another year. It had been some time since Tangier had achieved independence, which meant that there was no longer so much luxury, or so many foreigners remaining in the city, but the Dominguez family did stay. It was said that he — the father — was going to be named director of the Spanish branch where he had been working for some time.

At eleven, I was already drawing rather well and Fatima took me to the Pillars of Hercules (some caves by the sea) to see the beautiful scenery and make some sketches.

I felt like I was part of the setting, of those people, of those smells, so much that, although many years have passed, I still feel a deep, heartbreaking pain when I think about what had happened later and it is terribly difficult for me to recall it, trying, in some way, to put my ideas in order. It is as if an attempt were being made to revive someone who is no longer with us and continuing a battle with that spirit that, while now gone, still remains, deep down. Even now, another gust penetrates the window with an aroma of dates, palm trees, pistachios, and all mixed with those strong, sweet-smelling typically found in certain souks. This is an essential perfume, similar to the one in the salon where my aunt worked.

One Thursday afternoon I did not have school and Fatima washed me and did my hair carefully. She dabbed me with a little of the perfume she wore and kept in a big bottle covered with engraved arabesques on the glass. She pulled my Sunday clothes and well-polished dress shoes out of the wardrobe. The two of us walked towards the square and headed towards the place where my aunt worked. Climbing the ladder, I received the sweet smell as if it fell in large waves to welcome us. The lovely oak door was opened by a girl of about 18 — either Polish or Hungarian — whom I thought was very beautiful. Fatima did not pass through the door and I was left holding the girl's hand.

She gave me a chocolate she had kept in a wardrobe, an old Spanish-style piece of furniture, and accompanied me to a larger room which had two large mirrors facing each other. There, she had me sit on a red velvet couch and disappeared behind a door painted with strips of colours. I was sitting with my back to the door. I wanted to play and was looking at the lamp — which was like coloured glass balls; when my aunt came in, accompanied by an older man. My aunt was wearing a dusty-Parma-grey silk *negligee* or bed jacket that swung open when she walked. This revealed her white legs, on which she wore dark tights held with garters with a kind of smashed rose on each side. She was not wearing *panties* and I could see her short brown pubis. She did not seem embarrassed and chatted in a lively voice with the one geezer in Polish, I think. She served me some orange juice that was on the table which I had not noticed and left me with the old man without another word. He looked at me and asked me my age; I was eleven and told him so. He was very bald, had thin skin with little veins and short, greasy hands that were totally covered with rings. He smiled, and I could see two eyeteeth made totally of gold. He wore a European suit in with a vest (he had a huge belly) from which hung a watch with a gold chain. His arms were small and short and he seemed to move them like a toy, as if with springs. He stood me up and took off my panties himself and then my outfit, because I was not wearing anything else. I there I stood, totally naked. He began to stroke me with his hand as if he wanted to polish me; that moment lasted a very, very, very long time. He would stop and start over. I do not know how long we stayed like that with this strange game, but this coming and going all over my body had been going on for some time. Suddenly, he stopped and pulled a large, carefully folded handkerchief from his pocket; he unzipped his pants and covered the bottom part with the handkerchief. Right at that moment, my aunt came in and, without saying a word, took me out the room and helped me dress. After this, she took me to the house of a girl I had never seen before, and my aunt made multiple recommendations.

That evening, Fatima gave me some coins from my aunt and I went down to the bakery around the corner to buy myself a big cake. This was repeated every Thursday; it was always the same: Fatima accompanied me, I crossed the square with her and was it similar, exactly the same, always the same game with the same old and never a tender word, much less words of love; always the same coldness. Afterwards, there was a time when he would begin to rub me without a kiss, a caress or anything. He would his handkerchief out, my aunt would come and help me to get dressed, and I would return home accompanied by the maid.

At night, in my bed, I had a nightmare about the old man; I wanted a word of affection, a gesture of friendship or of tenderness towards my person. I hoped for it desperately, as only a child can hope for something. But every Thursday the same story was repeated, the same scene, the same coldness, the same alienation towards my person.

It was the Dominguez family who spoke with the Spanish priest. I do not know how or why, but they found out about my Thursday appointments. One day Madame Dominguez came by asking; she wanted to talk to my aunt. I was drawing in my room and I heard how Fatima told her that she was not in. They returned the next day and another until they finally found her, and then they talked for a while. Before a month had passed, my adoption papers were arranged; everything was ready. I said good-bye to the Dominguez family, then to my aunt. Fatima accompanied me to the ship that would take me to Spain and left me in the Captain's care.

The boat moved forward, creating playful waves as it moved, which I watched from the deck. The air smelled like sea and seaweed, and a feeling of happiness and freedom entered through my nostrils, filling my mind with well-being. I was sure that my life was going to change; uncertainty had not taken a toll on me; I was sure that everything would be fine, whatever my foster family was like. In reality, everything would depend on me, as always, and more and more every day more … and so it was.

THE LYING WOMAN (A STORY FOR ADULTS)

This is the story of a person who lies. And has done so forever. She was born that way. Her birth was a lie and since then, nothing has changed. Her name might be Maria and she might be thirty... or forty... or fifty. It is useless, because she has always lied about her age. She has also lied about her feelings and about her past. She could not lie about her future, because even she does not know or have a fixed idea about what is going to happen.

The story begins when she is about this age. She has been lying for some time. In order words, behind her is a long career of lying, to the point that she deceives herself about what is true and what is false.

This happens to her very often. Then she starts to look: She looks for someone to tell her the road, the path or the way of the truth. Naively, she deceives herself and always asks for the way from someone whom she should not ask. Then — well, let us call her Maria — she always takes a false path. It is not that she deceives herself, or that the people she asks — with good or ill will — do it. And so pass the days, from one deception to another. Maria has good intentions every morning. "Today I am not going to lie", but, after a while, she finds someone again asking questions, and she continues lying, continues inventing. One day, Maria met Frederic. He was from a foreign country, a South American. Frederic was wearing a tie and a business suit; he was serious. He smiled at Maria and spoke to her. Maria answered him with a smile. She has answered and he has spoken, and so has begun one of those love stories, or maybe a relationship between a man and a woman. And they have seen each other again, this time in Paris. He worked in a big skyscraper in a neighbourhood filled with businesses and then they have loved each other. At least, physically, yes. Maria would have liked to dare to ask him for a job, a job in the skyscraper, even if she just worked the switchboard. It was only that she was a liar, but not stupid. She could have asked for a job. No, a job is not impossible at your age. So, Maria was quiet. She would not get a job. It is from this moment — apparently unimportant — that Maria begins to understand. Maybe this is not so clear after all! Maybe it is her — the liar — who has always been the deceived. While it was not the words, but the stark reality, the facts. And this was even harder.

And, suddenly, things, facts, begin to change... Maria said that she came from a country in African. It was doubtful, but, without having studied it, she spoke Arabic. She said she had this or that, and to be this way or that way, and lived alone with her daughter at the edges of the society around her, reality. But, ultimately, what reality? The reality in her was as respectable as that of others, and no one can figure out where the real one starts to end the false one; only the end, the goal, the reason for fighting. The motive stayed always there, rock hard and solid, very solid. It was a search for total freedom, the true one, the only one, but... imagined, or really and truly real?

THE END OF THE STORY FOR GROWNUPS

ABOUT THE AUTHOR

Born in 1942 in Barcelona to a Spanish father and US-born mother, as far back as she can remember Cristina Roldán has always considered herself a fighter for freedom in general and for women in particular. She always says that she leads by example, and that that's the best way to do it. She divided her time between Paris (where she studied) and Barcelona until the age of 46, when she and her daughter Sarah left behind city, home and everything familiar to never return to live there again. Although Cristina has written in French and Spanish since she was a small child, she finished this novel in 1986. She never wanted to publish it until now, and it is now being published for the first time. Cristina is also a painter and has worked as one, with exhibitions worldwide, including three times at Paris' Grand Palace with the Société des Artistes Français under the pseudonym Mariah Rodriguez (www.mariahrodriguez.net). Cristina is the mother of three children and grandmother of seven grandchildren and has lived in Paris, Brussels, Barcelona, Madrid and London.

Printed in the United States
By Bookmasters

Printed in the United States
By Bookmasters